This
PJ BOOK
belongs to

PJ Library®

JEWISH BEDTIME STORIES and SONGS

To Debi, Mark, Addie, and Stephanie:
Dearest family, I hope you always
feel your best. God bless!
—K. W.

To Noah and Levi,
who once made me feel sick,
but now only ever make me feel better.
—J. C.

Margaret K. McElderry Books
An imprint of Simon & Schuster Children's Publishing Division
1230 Avenue of the Americas
New York, New York 10020

The text for this book is set in Adobe Caslon.
The illustrations for this book are rendered in acrylic paint.

Manufactured in China / 0613 SCP

2 4 6 8 10 9 7 5 3 1

Library of Congress Cataloging-in-Publication Data
Wilson, Karma.
Bear feels sick / Karma Wilson ; illustrations by Jane Chapman.—1st ed.
p. cm.
Summary: When Bear is too sick to play, his animal friends go to his cave to make him soup and tea and keep him company.
ISBN: 978-0-689-85985-4 (hardcover)
[1. Sick—Fiction. 2. Bears—Fiction. 3. Forest animals—Fiction. 4. Stories in rhyme.] I. Chapman, Jane, 1970– ill. II. Title.
PZ8.3.W6976Bc 2007
[E]—dc22
2004005297
ISBN 978-1-4814-0078-7 (proprietary ed.)

101322K1

Bear Feels Sick

Karma Wilson

illustrations by Jane Chapman

MARGARET K. MCELDERRY BOOKS
New York London Toronto Sydney

Alone in his cave
as the autumn wind blows,
Bear feels achy
with a stuffed-up nose.

He tosses and he turns,
all huddled in a heap.
Bear feels tired,
but he just can't sleep.

He sniffs and he sneezes.
He whiffs and he wheezes.
And the bear
feels
sick.

His friends gather round.
"Come out, Bear, and play."
Bear shakes his head.
"I'm too sick today."

Mouse mutters, “Oh my,
Bear’s head is too hot.”
Hare says, “We will help!
Here’s a warm, cozy spot.”

Bear mumbles and he moans. He grumbles and he groans.

And the bear
feels
sick.

Mouse squeezes Bear tight.
He whispers in his ear,
"It'll be just fine.
Your friends are all here."

Badger fetches water.
Gopher cooks the broth
while Mole soothes Bear
with a cool, wet cloth.

They cover Bear up and he drinks from a cup.

But he still feels sick.

Raven says, "*Caw!*
Come along, Owl and Wren.
Let us go gather herbs
to bring back to the den."

They coax Bear to sip
just a smidgen of tea.
"You'll feel better soon,"
says Mouse. "Wait and see."

Bear shakes and he shivers. He coughs and he quivers.

And he still feels sick.

The friends fuss and fret.
The friends cook and care.
They keep a close eye
on their poor sick Bear.

They all talk in whispers.
They walk on tippy toes.
They sing lullabies.
Then the bear starts to doze.

They watch Bear for hours.
"We've done all we could."

Then the bear wakes up.

And the bear feels GOOD!

Bear cries, “I’m all better.
I’m feeling like new.
I’m not hot and achy.
It’s all thanks to you!

"Let's celebrate now.
Let's go out and play.
Let's jump in the leaves.
Let's frolic all day!"

Then Mouse starts to wheeze and Hare starts to sneeze . . .

and the friends

feel

sick!

Bear murmurs, "Don't worry,"
and tucks them in bed.
He bundles them up
and he kisses each head.

He tells all his friends,
"You'll soon feel like new.
You took care of me . . .
now I'll take care of you."